Twelve Dancing Princesses

By the Brothers Grimm

Illustrated by Dennis Hockerman

This edition published in 2002.

Library of Congress Catalog Card Number: 78-18077

ISBN 0-8167-7514-1

Printed in China.

10 9 8 7 6 5 4 3

Once upon a time, a king had twelve beautiful daughters. Each night, he locked and bolted their bedroom door. But each morning, when he unlocked the door, he saw that his daughters had danced holes in their shoes. No one in the kingdom could explain it.

So the king said, "Anyone who can discover the secret in three nights can choose one of my daughters for a wife. In addition, he will rule my kingdom after I die. But anyone who tries and fails will lose his head."

Before long, a prince offered to try his luck. He was welcomed and treated royally. That night, he was led to the bedroom next to the one the princesses all shared. The doors were left open, so he might see where they went. But he grew weary and fell fast asleep. When he awakened, it was morning, and the princesses had

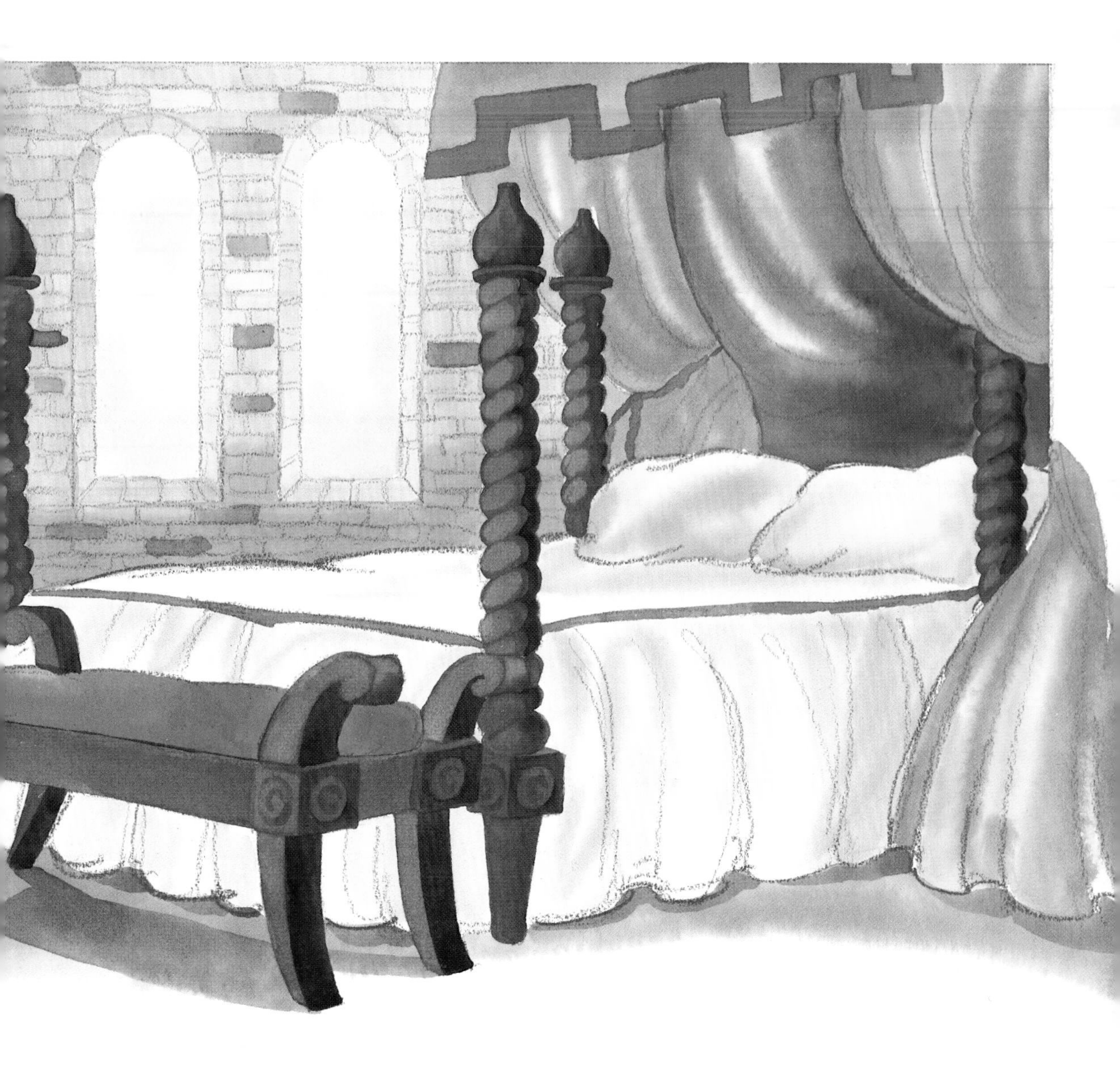

danced their shoes to pieces. On the second night, the same thing happened, and then again on the third. So the prince lost his head.

Many others tried to discover the secret of the twelve dancing princesses, but everyone who tried failed.

Now it came to pass that a poor soldier had suffered a wound and could not serve in the army anymore. He came upon an old woman, who asked him where he was going. ''I really don't know,'' he replied. Then he added, jokingly, ''Perhaps I will find out where the princesses dance holes in their shoes!''

"That is not very hard to do," said the old woman. "You must not drink the wine they will bring you each night. And you must pretend to fall into a deep sleep." Then she handed him a cloak and said, "This cloak will make you invisible, so you can follow the twelve princesses."

So the poor soldier went and offered his services to the king. He was treated just like the others. That night, the eldest princess brought him a cup of wine. But he had fastened a sponge under his chin. And instead of drinking the wine, he let it dribble down his chin into the sponge. Then he lay down and began to snore loudly, as if he were sleeping.

The twelve princesses heard him and laughed gleefully. Then they opened their closets, brought out beautiful gowns, and dressed themselves before the mirror. They whirled about, admiring themselves and eagerly looking forward to the ball.

But the youngest princess said, "Rejoice, if you will. But I have a strange feeling that misfortune will visit us tonight."

"What a silly goose you are!" replied the eldest.

"Have you forgotten how many princes have come here in vain? This poor soldier will fare no better than the rest. Why, even without a sleeping potion, he would have slept until morning!"

Then she went to her bed and tapped upon the bedpost. At once, the bed sank into the floor, revealing a long staircase. One after another, the twelve princesses went down the stairs.

Quickly, the soldier jumped from his bed. He drew on his cloak, which made him invisible, and followed them down the stairs. As he walked behind the youngest princess, he carelessly stepped on her gown.

"Wait!" cried the princess. "Someone is stepping on my dress!"

"Nonsense!" said the eldest. "You probably caught it on a nail."

They continued down until they were far underground. Then they came to an avenue that was lined with trees that had silver leaves. The soldier reached out and broke off a twig to keep as a token. But the youngest princess heard the snapping noise and became alarmed.

"Did you hear that?" she cried. "All is not well."

"Don't be silly!" replied the eldest. "It must have been a gun that was fired to salute us."

So they continued on, passing trees of gold, and then trees of diamonds. The soldier broke off two more twigs, and with each snapping sound, the youngest princess became alarmed. But each time, the eldest said that it was only a gun being fired in their honor.

Soon they arrived at a great lake, where twelve handsome princes were waiting with twelve little boats. The princesses seated themselves, and the soldier sat down in the boat with the youngest. The prince who was rowing it said, "I don't know why, but this boat seems

much heavier tonight. I must row with all my strength just to move it across the lake."

And the youngest princess said, "How strange! Perhaps it is the weather, for I feel very warm this evening, too."

On the opposite shore of the lake was a magnificent castle. From it came the glow of bright lights, and the sound of trumpets and drums drifted down to the lake. The princes rowed across to the castle and led the twelve princesses inside. When they danced, the soldier danced, too, but no one could see him. When one of the princesses raised her cup, the soldier drank what was in it. This upset the youngest princess, but the eldest silenced her, as usual.

By three o'clock, they had danced so much that they had worn holes in their shoes. Then they were rowed back across the lake, and the soldier sat in the boat with the eldest. The princesses said good night to the princes and promised to come back to the ball the following night.

As soon as they reached the steps, the soldier scrambled upstairs, took off his cloak, and lay down in his bed. As the princesses wearily reached the top of the stairs, they heard him snoring loudly. "Our secret is still safe, as far as he is concerned!" they said. Then they hung up their gowns, placed their worn-out shoes under their beds, and went to sleep.

The soldier did not tell the king what he had seen. Instead, he went with the princesses a second and a third time. Everything was exactly the same, except that on the third night, he brought back a wine goblet as a token.

After the three nights had passed, it was time for the soldier to give his report to the king. He took with him the twigs and the goblet. The twelve princesses hid behind a door, near enough to hear every word.

Then the king asked the soldier which of the princesses he would choose for a wife. And the soldier answered, "I am not as young as I used to be. Therefore, I will choose the eldest." And so the soldier married the princess, and the kingdom was promised to him upon the king's death.